SOLAS

A Tale in Three Parts

By the same author...
The Three Sorrows of Irish Storytelling.

Biblical Latin quotation in Text—Matthew 6.24.

Design, lettering and illustration by Frances Breen.

SOLAS

Thomas Campbell

Ogham Press

Part 1

In Ireland long, long ago there lived a holy monk named MacCu, who had an unholy love of learning.

When he wasn't tending his herb garden and vegetables, he read all day and wrote far into the night, until the rush-lights in his stone hut were used up. Then he staggered, weary and bleary eyed, to bed.

Over the years, the strain on MacCu's eyes from working in poor light took it's toll and he began to have difficulty in reading. It seemed as if he was looking through a fog and the words and lines on the page became jumbled together. This troubled him, as he knew that if he could no longer read and write he would die———.

MacCu lived on a sea-girthed island off the west coast of Ireland. But his solitude did not weigh heavily upon him, as he lived with the seasons, the rising and falling of the wind and the scudding clouds that came in from the west. Round him was the constant company of the sea. Sometimes in late Autumn, stirred by the wind, the sea raged and writhed around his island. But the shoreline, held by rocks that stood black, glistening and scarred by ancient wars with the elements, withstood the mighty force. More often the waters brimmed gregariously round his home and brought him driftwood for his fire and fish to eat.

The west side of the island was completely covered with rocks, but the sheltered east side had some flatland and soil. Years before, when MacCu had decided to make his home there, he had first cleared away and made fertile with sea-weed an area for growth. Here, on the east side, he had built his stone hut; and, sheltered by walls, he grew vegetables and had a herb garden.

The old monk now also had two goats, one of which he milked. But these animals were a mixed blessing. Generally they grazed upon green patches they found between the rocks and even feasted upon sea-weed. But sometimes, to supplement their diet, they made swift and furtive raids into MacCu's garden. These excursions into forbidden territory brought the holy monk roaring to the doorway of his hut, and the two goats— kicking their heels high into the air and with sprigs of green still sticking from their mouths—fled in a hail of stones. He tethered the animals to a post at night but found them more and more difficult to catch——.

MacCu had visitors from the mainland from time to time. They came to trade for the healing potions he compounded from his herbs. They also brought news from the outside and letters from all parts of the known world. For MacCu, before he had retreated to his island, had travelled widely. In his youth his peregrinations had brought him to Monte Cassino, Rome and Constantinople and he now wrote to many men of learning like himself in these and many other places—and they swopped books and information between them.

The visitors never stayed long because they found no comfort as the island's exposure to the elements did not allow for excesses but reduced life to the spiritual purity of endurance. MacCu was delighted to see his guests, but he was also glad to see them leave; he was impatient to tackle the books they had brought and he found that people distracted him from his studies. All-together, on his wind—swept island home, he was content except for the growing problem of his failing eye-sight.

Then one day all this was changed by an adventurous visitor, who had hitched a ride on the back of an unwilling seagull. The bird made several attempts to rid itself of its passenger by flapping its wings, ruffling its feathers and diving and soaring suddenly. It even tried to eat the little creature. But the fly could walk upside down and was quick-moving and agile; it hopped from wing-tip to wing-tip, then it retreated to the tail of the bird ahead of the yellow, snapping beak.

Within reach of MacCu's island, with the sun high in the sky, the battle between the pair had reached its climax. After a ferocious onslaught of pecking the little stowaway had decided to seek shelter from the attacking beak under the wings of its carrier. The gull began to veer sharply in the air as it felt the itch of the fly's crawl into an area where its left wing joined its body. It had had enough and decided to take extreme measures; it flapped its wings wildly for a moment,

13

then dived at a steep angle for the ocean. It was going under and its little passanger thought this tactic unfair. Just as the gull broke the surface of the water in its dive, the fly — unruffled and a true survivor — hopped off its unfriendly carrier and serenly continued the short flight to MacCu's island.

For some time the old monk did not know he had a visitor. But later that day, as he sat head bent outside his hut, a book open upon his palm, a fly landed on the page in front of his nose. He watched the little creature make its slow progress along a line of writing and suddenly realized that, as it walked along the page, it high-lighted and separated each word. This little creature, if properly trained, could help him with his reading and writing.

MacLu cupped his right hand carefully over the insect. The fly tried to escape, but it was tired after its flight with the gull and a later encounter on the island with the two goats. Eventually it settled and got assurance from the warm nest of the holyman's clasped palm. Carefully the monk placed the fly back on the book and looked at his captive through the bars of his fingers. He began to move the insect with his thumb along the page. In this way, back and forth, he marched the unwilling creature for several hours until it began to realise it could only walk with freedom just below the written line——.

16

MacLu kept the fly in a leather bag over-night
and began training it again the next morning.
And so it went on until eventually the monk could
take away his hand and the fly, instead of taking
off, happily marched across under the written line,
then down to the next line and so on to the end
of the page. MacLu had himself a self-propelled
pointer and became very fond of the little creature.
He called it Solas, which means light in Irish.
This language, invented by a wily and imaginative
people, did not have a word for "no". Because of
the endless possibilities this over-sight allowed,

Irish totally confused the devil and it was the only tongue he had despaired of learning. So by conferring on his guiding light a title in Irish the holy monk thought to protect the little insect from all harm by keeping it on the blind side of the devil. The fly also became very fond of the old monk and would not leave him but nested in his long white beard when he fell asleep.

The pair made a good team and worked long hours together, though Solas did not enjoy the task of guiding MacCu's quill pen across the unlined vellum page. The old monk's hand was unsteady and several times the fly was nearly written off as it was deluged by a sudden down—pour of ink. In other ways, too, the job was highly dangerous, and the lessons Solas had learned on the gull's back were put to good use as it hopped skillfully away

from the sharpened point of

a carelessly wielded

goose quill.

The old monk was happy with his new assistant. Now he felt blessed by the limits of his island. His own life became more ordered; he no longer tried to work far into the night as he did not want to over—tire his little helper. The old conflict with time was resolved : each dawn was a new beginning with tasks that filled exactly one day. Solas, from the air, even spotted the troublesome goats for the old monk and by flying round his head warned him of their approach to raid his garden.

After some time working as a pointer, Solas began to read. MacLu sometimes left the fly standing at a full stop when he had to chase the goats. From this, Solas learned that this point put an end to something. Under its feet was a world, seasoned and preserved by words, where—unlike life—nothing happened by chance. Solas became impatient to enter this world and grew tired of the interruptions that drew its master away. One day the little fly decided to venture on on its own and, using the manifold lenses of its eyes, it stepped beyond the reality of its life——

It climbed all over an N,
  it planted its feet on an E,
    it mounted the backs of an M,
      and (when it knew what it meant)
        it went into orbit round an O.

NEMO ... that's what it was ... NO MAN

At first the fly's progress at reading was slow and MacCu did not even notice that it had moved on when he returned to take up reading his book. But gradually the gaps became wider; Solas had moved on down the page or sometimes, if a breeze came from the right direction, had hopped over to the next page. As his eye-sight deteriorated, the old monk's dependence on his self-propelled pointer became greater; he now placed complete trust in the fly's position on the page and faithfully followed its progress as it moved on. But after some time using this method, he often found it difficult to make sense of what he was reading.

The old scholar prided himself on his logic and loved reading the philosophers. Despite the handicap of poor eye-sight, he knew instinctively that something was wrong. Previous to this, when immersed in a great work, he often sat back, reflected, and sighed with contentment as he allowed the grace and coherence of the philosopher's argument to cleanse his soul.

Now he got angry with what he considered
Plato's inadequate definition of knowledge.
He even took issue with Aristotle's theory of
universals and nearly flung the work aside in
exasperation when he found himself stranded
with conclusions that the text, which he had
read with the aid of the fly, did not substantiate.

The old scholar pondered long over the missing links, and he sometimes doubted his own sanity and he sometimes doubted the sanity of the Greeks. It took him sometime to check his pointer and tumble to exactly what Solas was doing. After that, whenever he had to leave off reading, he left a pebble as a marker on the vellum page. Then, when he returned to his book, he took no more nonsense but with an admonishing finger made the mischievous fly go back to the marked spot.

But in spite of having to wait for MacCu, the little creature's knowledge increased in leaps and hops. It forgot its lightness in air and liked instead being left alone in the hut with the books. When the old monk went outside, a book he had been using relaxed, stretched its spine, and often fell open at a page as if to display to the world what it knew. Solas, hovering above it waiting for such an opportunity, immediately alighted on the smooth, shining surface and began to read.

Always the explorer, the little fly loved maps and sometimes took a short flight across the page to Africa and spent an hour travelling along the course of the river Nile. One day it wandered far out on a blue painted ocean, fell asleep, and dreamed it had discovered.... a continent. Another day, Maclu returned to find Solas enclosed in a circle drawn by Ptolemy to explain his theory of the movements of the planets. As the old scholar watched it rubbing its tiny legs together with delight, he felt that the fly knew exactly where it was:
at the centre of everything, where
the spider used to be.

Part 2

There was at that time in Ireland another holy monk, who had an entirely different view of the world to that of the studious pair on MacCu's island. He was called Stone Mad. This was not his real name, but people had called him this for so long that he had forgotten what he had been named as a child.

Stone Mad was known all over Ireland because he was hell-bent on getting to heaven before his time. He was a builder and greatly admired a man called Simeon, who had spent thirty years on top of a sixty foot pillar near the city of Antioch in Syria. Stone Mad was more ambitious than Simeon: he wanted to go higher and perhaps reach heaven itself.

Unfortunately, Stone Mad's ambition had to contend with the people of Ireland. They liked to remain close to the ground and didn't like being looked down on; they also thought that if Stone Mad's building got too high, it would tear a hole in the sky and bring God knows what tumbling down on top of them. They liked their blue sky exactly the way it was and wanted the balance of nature to remain undisturbed. They also had no ambition to enter the next world before their time and resented Stone Mad's attempts to do so.

But, in spite of hostility, Stone Mad built. At first he miscalculated and ran out of building material before he had reached even the clouds. And his great structures were left towering over people.

But after much trial and error, he carefully selected a site so that he would have an endless supply of stone. Now, as people saw a structure emerging that was vaster and more complex than anything they had seen before, they feared that it would topple over and squash them. But Stone Mad was a good builder and loving his material he caressed each stone for strength and durability before putting it carefully in place. People came for miles to view the giant project as it went on and on. Looking up, they thought that each day the builder got nearer and nearer the sky. The crowd became uneasy and began to mutter among themselves. Something would have to be done.

It was impossible to identify who cast the first stone, but when it bounced harmlessly off Stone Mad's gigantic erection the crowd became ugly. A mob detached itself from the general assembly and suddenly rushed at the building and began tearing at its foundations with bare hands. When this had little effect, people became even more enraged as they imagined Stone Mad lolling at ease on top laughing at their puny efforts.

After some discussion, a more organised labour force was set up. Then tools and equipment were mustered and brought to bear on the stubborned foundation. Soon large boulders were levered away. As more and more people joined in the work, Stone Mad felt his whole structure give way under him. Eventually, he began to scramble down in fear of his life. The mob cheered in triumph as he lost his balance and slid uncermoniously down the last few hundred feet amid a pile of rubble. Shaken and bruised, Stone Mad got to his feet. He wanted to explain to people what they had destroyed, but seeing the mood of the crowd he lost courage and fled for his life.

After this, Stone Mad went from place to place leaving large piles of stones collapsed in his wake. People would not leave him alone; they allowed him to build up only so high before they gathered together and dismantled what he had constructed. Once a helpful poet, who had some sympathy with Stone Mad's quest, suggested to him that if he wanted to reach heaven, he should try climbing a mountain. Stone Mad thought there might be something in this and immediately set off for the nearest high mountain.

When he arrived at the base, the top of the mountain was covered by clouds. Stone Mad clapped his hands in excitement. Up there something was definitely going on! He was on the right track at last! Delirious with joy, he hoisted his habit and set off at a run hoping to get his head in the clouds. As the mountain became steeper, he was forced to slow down, but he still strode purposefully on___.

Eventually, Stone Mad had to rest. Gasping for breath, he sat down on a rock and stared fixedly and hopefully up the steep slope ahead. Now the wind had risen and the clouds were being carried away. Frantically the monk again set off — scrambling up the last of the slope and scattering loose stones in his haste. But, to his great disappointment, when he reached the summit, the clouds had cleared away and the sky seemed farther off than it had been from sea level.

Stone Mad sat down upon the mountain top to contemplate this problem. On his lofty peak he was surrounded by blue unbounded space: below him gulls wheeled and dipped their wings in eddies of air, to the north and south lay lower mountain ranges, to the east spread acres of green landscape, and to the west lay the great ocean, with its many islands —on one of which, far out, working in gentle and happy harmony, lived MacCu and Solas, his fly. But Stone Mad had climbed beyond his vision and he saw none of these things; his mind aspired only upwards and his thoughts drifted after the disappearing clouds.

After meditating for some considerable time, the monk concluded that God did not want him to reach heaven by this easy route and had deliberately lifted the sky just before he, Stone Mad, had reached the top of the mountain. He decided to wait and see if God would get tired of the game and let the sky slip down again.

Hours past, night fell and the stars came out — high, sparkling and wonderful.
The moon floated enticingly by, but it too kept its distance. Dawn came, the hard-boiled sun rose and, staring contemptuously down on the lone vigil of the monk, it kept the clouds away. It was going to be a long wait.

But after forty frustrating days, the only significant change Stone Mad observed in his celestial world was in the moon: it had become smaller and finally disappeared altogether. When he got up there, the monk resolved, he would put things right and restore it to its former burnished glory.

But eventually hunger and thirst drove Stone Mad down from the mountain top. During his time there the sky had remained exactly where it was; there was no easy route to heaven: he would have to build his own great structure from sea-level up. This way, he would approach heaven from an unexpected angle: God might have the mountains covered, but He couldn't watch everything.

After this, just as MacCu before him had retreated from the world to construct his house of knowledge, Stone Mad went further and further into the wilderness to build. But this withdrawal did not protect his giant sky-scrapers, as Ireland is a small country and sooner or later someone would spot a mountain of stones rising above the horizon where no mountain had been before.

What happened after that was always the same. As soon as the news spread that Stone Mad was at it again, a crowd would gather. Sometime later the monk, from the top of his mountain of stones, would see a mob heading in his direction. On arrival at the base, the work of destruction would begin. Several men would lever away the large boulders which had been strategically placed to support the foundations, then other stones would slip.

On the top, Stone Mad would hear a distant rumble within the giant structure he had built beneath him. In fear and trembling, he would begin to shout and scream at the mob as he felt once again the foundations of his stairway to heaven being undermined. If only there was

something he could clutch on to, but he wasn't
high enough, as round him was insubstantial
air that only the birds, with their angelic
wings, could make use of. If only the mob
could be made to understand, but it was no
use pleading with people and the more he
danced with rage the more enthusiastic they
became in dragging away his carefully
placed stones.

Soon the building would begin to slip and rumble even more as its foundations were shifted. All Stone Mad could do was to scramble down as fast as he could before The Crash. Sometimes, if the mob found it difficult to knock down his giant structures or if some of them were injured by falling rocks, they blamed him and became very angry. Then the holy monk had to flee for his life as his precious stones, thrown by the mob, came whizzing past his ears and bounced round his bare running feet.

After one such narrow escape from an angry crowd, Stone Mad, bruised and sore, limped away into the wilderness to think about what he should do. Things were not working out as planned; he couldn't get high enough because people were always knocking him down, if things went on like this he might not even survive long enough to get to heaven. One day, walking by the sea-shore, he thought of a solution: the safest

place for him to go was an island where there
was plenty of stone which he could use as
building blocks — and where no one would
bother him. He had heard of such a place
and of the tolerant scholar who lived there.
Pleased with the simplicity and perfection of
his plan, he found a suitable tree trunk and
began the long job of hacking, burning and
shaping it into a dug-out canoe.

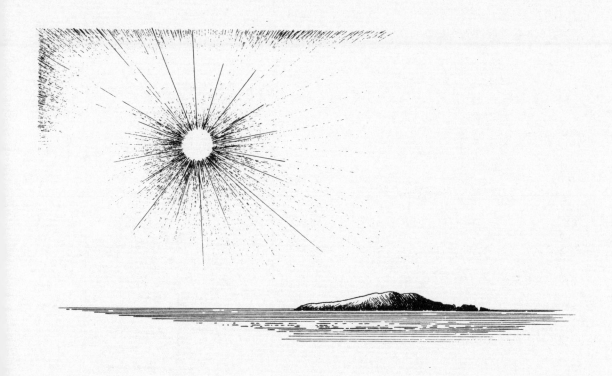

Part 3

And so it was that MacCu, one misty morning, as he was returning from his well carrying a brimming bucket of water, saw a stranger in a black canoe come riding in on the waves. The old monk, his left arm outsretched to balance his load, stopped to watch the stranger tie his boat to a rock; then, leaving his bucket, he went forward to greet his guest.

Stone Mad saw MacCu coming across the strand and busied himself unloading his tools and provisions. When the old monk reached him, he turned and in a voice that brooked no argument announced:

"I am Stone Mad, I have come to build."

Then abruptly he turned, shouldered his load, and set off along the shore line to a place some distance from MacCu's stone hut.

56

The old monk would have liked some further discussion with Stone Mad, as from visitors he had heard of the builder's ambition to get to heaven before his time. But, for the present, he decided to leave his guest alone: he himself enjoyed being on the earth and of the earth and would take heaven when it came in its own good time, he also doubted that Stone Mad, at least in his present mood, would appreciate a theological debate on the implications of his quest. MacCu returned to pick up his bucket, then slowly made his way to his hut: having glimpsed something ancient, inflexible and hard in the depths of his visitor's eyes, he felt a vague disquiet. Already, behind him, he could hear the dull clunks as Stone Mad placed stone upon stone.

After a week, MacCu could take the noise of building no longer; it went on every day from dawn until well into the night and it interfered with his reading and writing.

He couldn't concentrate on anything, although Solas, his little assistant, still marched happily along the lines of his book. In exasperation, the old monk went to Stone Mad to plead with him to at least take a rest.

When he reached the building site, he was surprised at the width and solid nature of the foundations. He was even more taken aback by the height the crazy builder had reached: he looked up ... then up again at the amazing structure. Every loose stone and boulder within easy reach had been moved and made use of in the building. Stone Mad was on top securing more stones he had hauled up. MacCu shouted to attract his attention, but was ignored. The monk then tried to climb the tower, but he was stiff with age and the stones were fitted so close that they offered few footholds.

Stone Mad used rope ladders when coming down and he always kept these drawn up when he was in residence on top. Even the two goats had failed to scale the steep sides of the building and had to content themselves with butting the base. However, Stone Mad kept a wary eye on the activities of these formidable animals as sometimes, when he was about to begin his climb and was at his most vulnerable, they appeared out of nowhere and made vicious assaults on his unprotected rear. Despite his enthusiasm for heights, the builder did not welcome this unwarrented assistance in his ascent towards heaven.

ventually MacCu, having failed even to get Stone Mad to acknowledge his presence, departed—leaving behind some food he had brought. The old monk had no fear that the building would get so high that it would tear a hole in the sky; his observations of the stars had led him to believe that if heaven was

up there it was a very long way off indeed.
However, he did think that if Stone Mad
continued constructing the way he was doing,
the building would be blown down by high winds
or it would eventually just topple over of its
own accord. But he did worry about the
amount of stone that was being used up;
if too much was moved, his island would be
washed away by the eroding tide.

Over the next few weeks the building continued. The structure had now reached such a height that even the sound of building was dulled, but it cast its shadow every bright sunny morning across the full length of the island. MacCu was finding it more and more difficult to read: just when he settled into a book he was roused by the sound of a carelessly placed rock that came crashing down from the monstrosity that was taking over his island. At first he tried to ignore what was happening, but every time he took a walk, he saw that even more stone had disappeared into the ever consuming tower. The landscape was changing its appearance; the goats now had fewer hiding places and the sea was making its way further and further inland—in many places there were now pools of water where once rocks had been embedded.

MacCu tried to become friendly with Stone Mad by leaving him food. But the builder never came down to eat until he knew that the old monk had gone away. Only Solas, the fly, seemed unaffected by the changes Stone Mad had wrought on the island. The little creature was now totally absorbed in the piles of books in the stone hut; it endured with Xenephon and

his men on their epic anabasis, it stood with
Socrates before his accusers and nimbly followed
his defence along the scripted line. Every morning
Solas would waken MacCu by crawling on his
closed eyelids and would give the scholar no
peace until a book was opened. Every evening
the old monk had to coax the fly away from
its academic search for the meaning of life
and toss it in the air to help him locate the
goats.

As he felt it more difficult to concentrate on his reading, MacCu spent more time fishing off the rocks on the west side of the island. Here at least he was away from the disturbance caused by the building. One evening he returned, carrying two mackeral for his supper, to find that the walls he had built to protect his garden had disappeared and the two goats were greedily eating in the middle of his vegetables. Stone Mad was running out of moveable material to use in his demonic colossus and he was now taking anything he could lay his hands on.

MacCu went to the tower to remonstrate with the thief. But the series of rope ladders that Stone Mad used to climb the lower part of the building were drawn up and the vast mountain of stones was now so high that its builder could neither be seen nor heard. Sadly the old monk retraced his steps to drive the goats from what remained of his garden. The peace of his island home on the far margin of the world had been destroyed and soon, he realized, even his stone hut would be used as building material in Stone Mad's crazy attempt to get to heaven before his time.

The next morning, after a long sleepless night, MacCu —driving the goats in front of him— again set out to the west side of the island. There at least he could think about his situation in peace. He had begun to hate the sight of the ever rising tower, inhuman in its scale, enterprize and devouring power. He had stopped leaving food for Stone Mad in the hope of starving him out. But the builder had long been used to living off the land and descended from his lofty perch every so often to forage for mussels and other shell-fish that grew in abundance on the rocks.

When the old scholar reached his destination, he settled himself on a flat rock that had been too large for Stone Mad to move. From here he could keep an eye on the goats and prevent them from returning to devour the last of his vegetables. He could feel the heat of the sun on his shoulders as it rose in the sky. Below him a blue, grey and silver sea stretched as far as the eye could see. He wondered what was out there to the west beyond the horizon on the far rim of the world, he wondered if there was another exit. But the old monk knew, with the finality of a lifetime, that his way of life was ending.

He would soon have to leave his island home, but he was too old and his eye-sight too weak to start again elsewhere. Solas, the fly, had extended his reading life and kept the darkness at bay, but he doubted if either of them would last much longer. He wondered if his destiny was to have to lie down weeping in darkness. Thinking about what he should do, the old man dozed off, as the sun — now high in the sky — warmed his body.

Back on the east side of the island, Stone Mad had watched MacCu leave. As soon as the old monk was over the ridge, the builder, knowing he could not be seen, descended from his tower and stealthily made his way to his stone hut. The old scholar's home contained the only moveable stones left on the island and Stone Mad immediately began to dismantle it. All day he laboured knocking and then carrying stones away to his tower. There he loaded them on a wooden platform, made from his canoe, and hauled them up to the top with ropes.

StoneMad was still sure that if he could find enough material to build high enough, he would eventually step off into heaven itself and be absorbed in its glory. But by evening all the stones that had been in the hut had been lifted to his tower and he still had not reached the sky. The only thing now remaining on the island that he could move and build with was MacCu's vast pile of books that lay — exposed, now that the hut had been removed.

All day Solas, the fly, had been reading one of its favourite books —— the Bible. As Stone Mad was removing parts of the hut, the book became open to the wind and the pages were turned sometimes so quickly that the fly was scarcely able to finish reading one page before another heavy vellum page fell like a blanket on its back. Still, the little creature was enjoying the freedom to read that the wind and the light allowed.

Stone Mad began taking away the piles of books and drawing them up into his tower. Solas was aware of the stranger moving about and removing the books, but the fly had long ceased to care about the world outside the one it was reading about. Now the wind turned the page to the verse beginning with the first word whose meaning the little creature had penetrated. It felt the old thrill of excitement and trepidation as it crawled along under the words . . . . .

".......... NEMO POTEST duobus dominis servire... "

Then it saw the stranger's shadow darken the page. Its instincts warned it of danger and it tensed its tiny legs to fly.

But it was too late! Stone Mad reached down and, without even seeing the little creature, soundly closed the book on the fly. He then set off, with the Bible under his arm, back to his tower.

When all the books had been brought
to the top, the builder began to stack the volumes
carefully on the stone. He had never built with
books before; they were less reliable than stone.
The wind from the west had risen and was
now sweeping across the island in gusts
that hit the tower with ever increasing force.

Stone Mad thought he could sometimes feel
his great building sway under him. He found
it increasingly difficult to keep his balance in
the high wind and, looking down far below
him, he saw the sea become choppy and
tufted with white.

As the pile got higher, the builder had to climb on top and pull the last of the books up by rope. Surely heaven could not be far off! As the evening drew in, the sky seemed very close! Stone Mad placed the large Bible, containing the crushed body of Solas, under his feet and stood upright. Suddenly the column of books became unstable and began to wobble. Then the whole pile gave way under him.

Stone Mad was falling down, down.... then a gust of wind hit his tower with terrific force and it too keeled over and came Tumbling after him. With a great splash, the whole lot hit the sea. Carried by the weight of the stones that were now falling all round, Stone Mad went down, down.... then down again into the depths of the ocean. Eventually he hit the bottom, but then a part of his tower came hammering down on top of him and he went further still....

Some say he fell, fell
Down into hell, hell.

More say he went further still....

That he went pell-mell
Further than hell.

Will he build up again?
will he build up again?
... .. build up again.

On the west side of the island, MacCu, still lying on the flat rock, when he heard the crash, awoke with a start. He knew immediately what the rumbling noise had been, as Stone Mad's hated tower had disappeared from the sky-line. He hurried back. As he came over the ridge that divided the island, he saw what remained of the giant structure lying stretched out like a pathway leading into the sea. Already the two goats were gambolling triumphantly on its rocky surface. Then, as the old monk came closer to the scene of destruction, he saw that his stone hut was missing and that his books were gone.

MacCu walked to the shore line and, staring out, could just make out some of the books he loved floating in the sea. Then, as they became water-logged, they too sank. Stone Mad and Solas were nowhere to be seen and the old scholar guessed what had happened. When he realized that his home and all that he had loved had gone, the old monk sank to his knees and — stretching his arms out — prayed for enlightenment.

The west wind billowed his habit and his grey hair flew around, but otherwise the holy man remained motionless in his cross-vigil position for a long time and he saw the world for what it was: under him the sharp stones cut at his knees, behind him the light faded, before him was the unrelenting sea—a whole civilization lost beneath its waves. Against all this the monk had his sober faith.

Eventually his arms dropped to his side, then he raised them and bowed his head into his hands and covered his ears in anguish at the terrible silence of God. Again, for a time, he remained kneeling and motionless. Then slowly he raised his head and two welled up tears ran from his sightless eyes into his white beard. Darkness had descended upon MacCu.

Published by Ogham Press, 90 Eaton Wood Grove,
Shankill, Co. Dublin, Ireland.

ISBN 1 869956 02 8.

This book has been grant-aided by Telecom Eireann.

Printed by Printwell Co-op, Dublin. Tel: 771507